T0198974

THE
DRAGONSLAYING
FARMER

By W.D. Correia

WestBow Press books may be ordered through booksellers or by contacting:

WestBow Press
A Division of Thomas Nelson & Zondervan
1663 Liberty Drive
Bloomington, IN 47403
www.westbowpress.com
1 (866) 928-1240

ISBN: 978-1-9736-7298-2 (sc)
ISBN: 978-1-9736-7299-9 (e)

Library of Congress Control Number: 2019912536

Print information available on the last page.

WestBow Press rev. date: 9/17/2019

WestBow
PRESS®
A DIVISION OF THOMAS NELSON
& ZONDERVAN

Dedicated to:
RUTH YSABELLA
my little myth writer!

A long time ago, in a faraway land, filled with green hills and dark forests, was the kingdom of Astril. This kingdom was ruled by a wise and just King and a kind and beautiful Queen. Their subjects loved them because they protected the weak, cared for the orphans, and were swift in giving justice.

They had one child; a daughter named Mirella. She was wise like her father and even more beautiful than her mother, with long red hair and emerald eyes.

Everyone in the kingdom loved the royal family of Astril; except one — the dragon, Volt. He lived in the black hills of Ustana and his hatred was as foul as the yellow breath seeping through his black teeth.

One day, he thought of a plan to bring pain and sadness.

"I know what I will do," Volt said, his red scales glistening in the sun. "I will burn the kingdom to the ground and steal the Princess. I will keep her, giving them the hope that they can rescue her. Let them try, but they will all fail. And when there is no one else to rescue her, I will eat her!"

When the sun began to set, Volt flew down with wide wings like an oversized bat. The sound of his arrival was like that of a hurricane, followed by fire and smoke. Screams filled the air. He circled the kingdom with Mirella in his grasp for all to see, before flying off to his lair.

The King and Queen summoned for help from other kingdoms. They tried their best to help their subjects, but the missing Princess was on their heart. Many times, the King wept openly, and the Queen would lock herself in her chamber for days.

A decree went out from the King:

> To all the knights in the realm: whoever rescues Princess Mirella and kills the dragon, bringing his head, I will make him a lord of the kingdom and, if the princess wishes it, give her hand in marriage.

Several knights attempted to rescue the Princess. Few returned. Many did not.

One brave knight, wounded by Volt, fell off his horse onto a field. A young farmer named Frederick saw him while plowing his fields and carried him home to nurse his injuries. The knight described his battle with the dragon and said it was impossible to defeat him. The next day he died. The farmer gave the knight a proper burial in the place where he found him.

Frederick pondered about what the knight told him. He remembered seeing the Princess in a royal procession when he went into the city to sell his crops. He grieved for the King and Queen for losing their child.

"But I'm only a simple farmer," he said. "There's nothing I can do."

He glanced at the armor on his kitchen table. Only knights have been called to rescue the Princess and the punishment for impersonating a knight was death. He wasn't trained for battle, but he had fought off wild beasts attacking his father's flocks when he was a child. His years of farm labor made him strong and able to withstand hardship better than most men — even knights. Therefore, he put on the armor and mounted his plow horse, Tommy.

After traveling through swamps, forests, and ravines, he reached the black hills of Ustana. He knew he arrived at the right cave when he heard the dragon's growling snore and Mirella's whimpering. He noticed a great boulder resting above the cave's entrance and thought of a way to defeat Volt. He climbed up to the boulder and tied a rope around it and attached the other end to Tommy's harness. He knew his horse would have no trouble moving it since Tommy was used to pulling heavy loads.

The farmer stood in front of the cave's entrance with shield and sword, shouting, "Volt! Come out and fight!"

A terrible roar with yellow smoke belched forth as Volt bolted out of the cave. He aimed a stream of fire at Frederick, who crouched behind his shield.

"Now, Tommy! Pull!"

Tommy heaved forward and moved the boulder with ease, causing it to fall on top of the dragon, pinning him to the ground. Volt scraped at the ground trying to free himself but without success. The farmer leaped forward and with one swing of his sword he cut off the dragon's head.

Later, Frederick entered the royal city with Princess Mirella riding Tommy as he dragged the head of the dragon behind him. The whole kingdom came out to see the glorious sight and erupted into shouts of joy. As he reached the palace, the King and Queen ran out to embrace their daughter, thanking Frederick for saving her and destroying Volt.

However, one group of people were not celebrating: a small crowd of jealous knights, watching in the distance. They had never heard of a knight named Frederick and decided to check his name against the Royal Register.

In the great cathedral, with its tall columns, grand arches, and brilliant stained-glass windows, Frederick walked down the aisle, with nobles and commoners standing on either side. But before the King could bestow lordship on him, the jealous knights stormed in with shouts of 'fraud' and 'imposter,' saying that Frederick was not a knight.

The King peered down at Frederick and asked, "Is this true?"

"Yes, it is."

Gasps and murmurs filled the cathedral.

Frederick told of the wounded knight who later died and how he struggled with the decision to rescue the Princess.

"Why would you risk your life to battle Volt and to impersonate a knight?" the King asked.

Frederick hung his head and sighed.

"Did not the true King of this cathedral, wearing a crown not of gold but of thorns, give his life for you and me? Therefore, it was good and right to sacrifice my life for another." He knelt before the king, preparing for his judgment, bearing his neck.

"Then I must do what I must."

The King unsheathed his sword and raised it up.

The crowds shouted and cried.

The knights grinned.

But instead of a deathly blow, he gently placed the sword on one shoulder and then the other.

"Arise, Sir Frederick, Grand Knight and now Lord of the kingdom of Astril."

Cheers erupted throughout the cathedral.

The knights objected. "What? Why?"

"You vile men!" the King said with fiery eyes. "This man's character and deeds showed that he was already a knight. But your actions have revealed your wickedness and cowardice. Your knightship is revoked. Guards! Imprison them until I decide their fate."

The knights cried as they were dragged away.

The King and Queen approached their daughter and asked if she would be willing to marry him, to which she agreed.

Several years later, Lord Frederick and Princess Mirella became the King and Queen of Astril, and throughout the land, everyone said that they were the wisest and most just rulers Astril ever had!

THE END

Printed in the United States
By Bookmasters